F
FE   Ferguson, Alane

            The practical joke
              war

$12.95   91-207

DATE			

The Practical Joke War

by Alane Ferguson

Bradbury Press / New York
• • • • • • • • • • • • •
Collier Macmillan Canada / Toronto
Maxwell Macmillan International Publishing Group
New York / Oxford / Singapore / Sydney

ALSO BY ALANE FERGUSON
Cricket and the Crackerbox Kid

For older readers
Show Me the Evidence

Bradbury Press
Macmillan Publishing Company
866 Third Avenue
New York, NY 10022

Collier Macmillan Canada, Inc.
1200 Eglinton Avenue East
Suite 200
Don Mills, Ontario M3C 3N1

First edition
Printed in the United States of America
1 2 3 4 5 6 7 8 9 10

The text of this book is set in 14 point Caledonia.
Book design by Cathy Bobak

Library of Congress Cataloging-in-Publication Data
Ferguson, Alane.
The practical joke war / Alane Ferguson — 1st ed.
p.   cm.
Summary: The Dillon children's practical jokes on each other grow
and increase to a breaking point where they are finally drawn
together in friendship.
ISBN 0-02-734526-2
[1. Practical jokes—Fiction.   2. Brothers and sisters—Fiction.]
I. Title.
PZ7.F3547Pr   1991   [Fic]—dc20   90-45578

*To Ron, who loves my
jokes almost as much as I do*

The flame of the candle flickered for an instant, then went out. Smoke curled around the blond lady's hair.

"We mustn't be frightened," she whispered to the scientist.

"But we are deep in Pharaoh's tomb, and now we have no light. Wait!" the scientist exclaimed. "Do you hear that strange, eerie growling?"

"Scared yet?" eleven-year-old Taffy Dillon asked her little brother, Eddy.

She and Eddy had nestled into the couch with popcorn and corn curls and a big bag of M&M's. Russell, their big brother, was getting 7-Up from the kitchen.

"Naw, I'm not scared," Eddy told her. He popped a piece of candy into his mouth. "These old movies are dumb. The mummy's gonna eat the scientist, then try and marry the blond lady. Dumb, dumb, dumb."

Taffy nodded. "Yeah, nobody could get spooked watching this old stuff."

Still, as the TV mummy crept through the shadows, Taffy felt her heart beat a little faster. The mummy didn't have eyes. Instead, he looked as though two holes had been poked right in his face. He grunted a lot. Drool hung from the corner of his twisted mouth.

"Boo!" Eddy yelled.

"Aaack!" Popcorn flew from the bowl Taffy held. It sailed through the air and landed all over the couch, like a popcorn blizzard.

"Oh, real funny, Eddy. You can just clean this mess up."

"No way! You're the one who did it. Were you *scared*!" He wiggled his fingers in her face. "The mummy's gonna get you. Oooooh!"

"Shut *up*! We're missing the show."

Crossing her arms, Taffy scooted deep into the cushions. She wriggled her backside, frowned, then pulled a handful of popcorn from beneath her bottom. Eddy snickered. Rolling her eyes, Taffy sighed. It was awful being the only girl in the Dillon family. Eddy was nine years old and a pain half the time, plus he was a boy. And Russell was one year and three months older than she so he thought he knew *everything*. The only person in the whole world she really felt close to was her new best friend, Susan. When Susan had moved into their neighborhood a month before, they'd become instant friends. The mummy movie would have been a lot more fun if Susan had been there, but tonight she was busy baby-sitting the Fagel twins. Taffy knew she was stuck with her brothers.

She looked over at Eddy. He was feeling around for lost kernels while keeping his pale eyes glued to the show. Both Russell and Eddy had sky blue eyes, along with dark, chocolate-colored hair and short, stubby noses.

Of course she, on the other hand, looked exactly like her name. Maple-taffy-colored hair. Maple-taffy-colored eyes. Even her lashes were the color of syrup.

"Move," Eddy commanded. "You're squashing the popcorn."

Taffy scooted over and tried to concentrate on the movie.

Along the wall of the tomb, arms stretched straight out, lurched the TV mummy.

"Behind you! Look behind you!" the blond lady screamed.

At that instant, the lights in the Dillon house went off. The picture on the television set disappeared, leaving a tiny dot at the center of the screen. Soon it, too, blinked away. The room was totally quiet. And dark.

"What happened?" asked Eddy.

"I guess the power's out. Russell, grab a flashlight," Taffy called toward the kitchen.

"You guys don't panic," Russell yelled back. "I'm knocking into everything 'cause I can't see. I know there's a flashlight in here somewhere."

It was nine o'clock at night. A large, full moon cast deep shadows both outside and in. The sliding glass doors were open to the screen, and in the June breeze the curtains puffed out and sucked in like muslin ghosts. Beyond the doors lay the backyard, then a fence, then a little stream, and then a field. None of the Dillon kids liked to go outside at night.

"*R-u-s-s-e-l-l,* hurry!" Eddy wailed.

"Just wait a second! I'm trying!"

"But it's *d-a-r-k!*"

Suddenly, Eddy pointed a shaking finger toward the curtains. "What was

5

that?" he squeaked. "I saw something!"

Eddy, who claimed that he was never scared, clung to his sister like a spider monkey.

"I didn't see anything. It's just the wind," Taffy told him. "Come on, squirt, be brave."

"But it was there! Honest! I don't care about brave, I'm gonna get Russell." He bolted from the couch and ran into the kitchen. "You gotta come out and be with us," Taffy heard him plead. "There's something weird in the backyard."

Pulling her knees to her chest, Taffy suddenly felt very alone in the family room. Carved wooden ducks looked strangely mean, as if they could peck her with their sharp, wooden beaks. And if she squinted, the plant in the corner seemed to move, just the tiniest bit, all by itself.

"Don't be a baby," Taffy scolded herself. "It's just your imagination. Things don't come alive in the dark."

She knotted her fingers. She took a

deep breath and blew it out slowly between her teeth. She bit her lip.

That's when she heard it. A scritching, scratching sound at the screen. Then slowly, so slowly, the screen door glided open. A white, bandaged hand slipped through, then another, then a leg, and then a face with black eyes sunk deep into its head.

"*Aaaaahhhhhhhh!*" Taffy screamed. Her hands flew to her mouth in horror. She knew she was about to die, to be chopped into small, edible pieces and fed through the little hole that was the mummy's mouth. She'd heard that before people died their lives passed before their eyes. But she'd only lived eleven short years. . . .

"*Ha ha ha ha ha ha ha!*"

Eddy rolled across the family room floor, howling with glee.

"Did you see her face?" he gasped to the mummy.

A muffled voice, *Russell's* muffled voice, replied, "I know. I thought her eyes would pop right out of her head. What a dork!"

Taffy felt her jaw clamp together. It was a *joke*! When Russell stepped closer, she could see that he was wound head to foot in white Ever Soft toilet paper.

"Russell, you *jerk*!" she shrieked.

"Had you going there, didn't I? I'm good. I'm *sooooo* good!"

"Creep! Slime!" Taffy lunged toward him, and as Russell tried to get away he tripped over Eddy.

"Scum! Dog spit!"

Suddenly it was hard to tell who was who. Bits of toilet paper floated through the family room as the three of them tumbled into a sibling ball. They were squealing, pulling, tossing until they heard the door bang open and saw two pairs of shoes stop in front of their eyes.

The low-heeled sable pumps belonged to their mother. The mushroom-colored running shoes were their dad's.

"RussellTaffyEddy, stop that right this minute!" cried their mother.

"Boys, get off your sister!" ordered their dad.

Taffy yanked her arm from underneath Russell's back and sat up. A piece of toilet paper stuck to her tongue. She pulled it out and rolled it between her fingers until it became a tiny ball.

"It was just a joke, Dad," Russell told him.

"Yeah," Eddy added, "a joke."

"A *joke*! Look at this room!" Their mother began to walk around, pointing as she went. "Toilet paper! M&M's! And just look at my couch! It's buried in popcorn!"

"A joke is supposed to be funny," added their father. "Do you see me laughing?"

"We leave you alone for one hour," their mother went on, "and just look what happens! How can I trust you alone all summer if you act like this when we're away?"

Eddy and Russell hung their heads. Taffy did, too. She was really truly sorry for the mess they'd made. And she knew they would all have to clean it up. She knew Russell and Eddy would promise never, ever to do it again. That would be nice, Taffy thought. Useless, but nice. She looked at her brothers from under lowered lashes and smiled a tiny, secret smile. Because she knew something neither one of them knew. Her brothers had banded together to play their last practical joke on her. Starting with Russell, she would make them pay. From now on, this was *war*!

...

"I hope you've learned something from all this," their father declared.

Taffy stacked the sofa cushions to one side, then turned on the vacuum cleaner. Flattened popcorn kernels rattled up the long hose. She stepped over Eddy, who was crawling on his hands and knees in search of lost M&M's.

"Sure, Dad," muttered Russell from the corner of the room.

Mummy strips curled around him like

11

a white, Ever Soft cloud. Scowling, he yanked the toilet paper into squares, then tossed them into a bag marked RUSSELL.

"And you will use those and nothing but those squares until every one of them is gone," said their mother.

"But *Mom,* I'll be using this stuff till I'm twenty-one!"

Smiling, she ruffled his hair. Their mom was pretty, Taffy thought. Not all angles and bones like some moms. "Fluffy" is how her mother put it. Smooth, coffee brown hair brushed the tip of her collar, and her eyes crinkled when she smiled. Because she was the principal of Canyon View Elementary, Mrs. Dillon knew a lot about kids. And about making them pay for their crimes.

From the plaid reclining chair their father said, "A tree gave its life for that toilet paper, son, and we just can't waste it. You know, I've got some wonderful material on ecology right here. . . ." He began leafing through papers piled next to him. "No, wait, it's upstairs. It's fasci-

12

nating reading. I'll get it for you."

Russell shook his head.

Their dad was a librarian, so almost every night he brought home "fascinating" magazines and books about saving the planet. If he wasn't working in their garden or tapping at his computer, their father could always be found reading. His gold, wire-rimmed glasses would slip down his thin nose; if he was really into a book, he'd begin to scratch at the edges of his gray-black beard. "You'll never be bored as long as you've got a good book," he'd say. Now that it was summer, he said that a lot.

"That's okay about the ecology stuff, Dad," Russell told him quickly. "I believe you."

"Oh. Well. If you're sure." Slapping his hands against his blue jeans, their father stood. "Say, guys, it's late. I suppose these jobs can wait till morning."

"Hallelujah," Russell muttered.

Taffy glanced around to make sure no one was watching. Carefully, so as not to

13

attract attention, she palmed a Ping-Pong ball and dropped it into her pocket.

"Can I call Susan?" Taffy asked. She had a great plan, and she wanted to bounce it off her friend first. Susan was encouraging her to think big, to try more things, to be daring. Susan would be proud of what Taffy had in mind tonight!

"I don't think so. It's already nine-thirty," her dad told her. "Why don't you wait till morning."

"Okay."

"But don't call too early," her mother added.

"All right." Taffy wasn't about to argue, not after her close brush with parental law. She could imagine what Susan would say, anyway.

"I'm proud to have a friend with such a devious mind," she'd say. Susan always said stuff like that, which was why Taffy loved to hang around her. Last week the two of them had decided that Taffy needed to jazz up her image.

They'd been at the mini-mall and had

stopped in front of a nail polish display.

"Pick a flavor," Susan had said.

Taffy had studied all the colors, the frosts and the creams, from the blood reds to the rows of soft peaches. She'd chosen a bottle marked Sandstone.

Susan had sighed. "I know this is a big step up from clear nail polish, but have you ever considered anything with *color* in it? This says an awful lot about your personality."

"What do you mean?"

"I mean I've just read this article that says the color of polish you choose reveals who you are. For example, I just picked Double Hot Pink. You picked that." She pointed to the small bottle with disdain. "The trouble is, you're too beige, Taffy. Inside, I mean."

The comment had stung, mostly because it was so true. Taffy had decided right then to try and change. She'd borrowed Susan's neon earrings, and she'd bathed herself in a perfume called Sin. She'd brushed her hair upside down, so it

15

had more pouf, and she'd even tried a little mascara, although she'd chickened out and washed it off before her parents came home. Still, she was changing. Now it was time to add some "color" to her personality. She was going to quit being mousy and get back at anyone who crossed her. And tonight, that anyone was Russell.

Stretching her hands above her head, she tried to sound sleepy. " 'Night, every-body."

"Good-night, dear. See you tomorrow."

Taffy walked out of the room slowly. It was important that no one suspect. What if, she worried, Russell didn't raid the re-frigerator before bed like he always did? Then there wouldn't be time to carry out her plan. She bit her lip. Russell had eaten tons of junk all evening long, and any nor-mal person would be stuffed!

"I'm hungry," Russell announced. "I think I'll grab some cereal."

Grinning gleefully, Taffy rounded the corner and bounded up the stairs to her room. Her cat, Furball, mewed at her from the middle of Taffy's pillow.

The room was as much the cat's as it was Taffy's. Rubber mice and string balls lay scattered across the floor, and the walls were covered with posters of big-eyed kittens. Russell referred to her room as "the litter box." He definitely preferred dogs.

Grabbing Magic Markers, scissors, and a hanger from her closet, Taffy hopped onto her bed and crossed her legs, Indian style. Furball rolled over and began to purr.

"You wonder what I'm up to, don't you?" she asked as she scratched the silky triangle of fur under his chin. "Revenge, my little Furball, revenge! Now, scoot. I've got to go to work."

Taffy held the Ping-Pong ball carefully and drew a black, pea-sized dot. Next she encircled the dot with a ring of lime green.

"Red! Drat, where'd I put the red?" She pawed through her markers until she found the right one. It took only a minute to squiggle scarlet lines all over the rest of the Ping-Pong ball. Finished, Taffy held it out and grinned. A perfect eyeball oogled back.

`This'll get him, she decided. I think Russell's forgotten just how sneaky I can be.

Glancing at the clock, Taffy suddenly realized how late it was. Eddy had already gone to bed, and Russell would be upstairs any minute.

"Move *over,* Furball, you're on my stuff."

She grabbed the hanger, unwound it from the top, then yanked and pulled until the wire was almost straight.

As quickly as she could, Taffy took the tip of her scissors and drilled a hole at the bottom of the eye. Then she popped it onto the wire.

"Perfect! Okay, cat, you stay here. I don't want your meowing to give me away."

Like Furball on a hunt, Taffy sneaked

down the hall and ducked into Russell's room. Socks, metal cars, blue jeans, old school papers, and a half-eaten sandwich lay scattered across the floor. The bed seemed to sag under a heap of clothes.

"Okay," a voice floated up. "I'm goin'."

Russell! Clutching her eyeball-on-a-wire, Taffy dove under the bed and tried not to breathe. Seconds later, she heard Russell walk in. The bed creaked as he lifted an armful of clothes off the mattress. After dumping them in a corner, he jumped onto the bed and kicked off his sneakers. They landed right next to Taffy's nose.

Uck, she thought, fish feet!

She'd heard rumors that other girls thought Russell was cute. He had a way of cocking his head and grinning so that all his teeth showed, and his black lashes made his big eyes look even bigger. She wondered what those girls would think if they smelled the insides of his sneakers!

Russell whistled. He sang the words to a rock song. Taffy tried not to giggle when his voice squeaked on the very highest notes. After what seemed like forever, he finally turned off the light and climbed under the covers.

The moon shimmered through the curtains. Russell threw himself from side to side before settling on his stomach. His hand dangled over the edge; the tips of his fingers barely missed Taffy's head.

Then Taffy made her move.

She wiggled out just far enough to see Russell's face. Without a sound she raised the wire and the bloodshot eye until it hovered over Russell's head. The Ping-Pong ball seemed to glow in the moonlight. Russell gave a little snort. Taffy waved the eyeball from side to side, like a windshield wiper. Finally Russell's lids fluttered open, then drifted shut again. He rubbed his nose.

Taffy sighed. This was going to be harder than she'd thought.

Suddenly, Russell's eyes snapped open again. A flash of plain fear crossed his face; he screamed higher than she'd ever heard him scream before.

"*H-e-l-p!* Mom, Dad, *h-e-l-p! Monster!*"

Leapfrogging to the middle of the bed, Russell yanked his covers under his chin. "Mom, Dad, *invasion! Help!*"

"I gotcha. Oh, I gotcha!" Taffy exploded. She scooted farther out, so that she wouldn't have to miss a thing. It was so *funny* to see her brother squeal like a stuck pig!

"What is it! What's wrong?!" The door to Russell's room knocked open with a bang. Their dad flipped on the light and looked around frantically.

From the bedroom floor, Taffy whispered, "Hi, Daddy." The eyeball-on-a-wire quivered in her hand.

Crossing his arms, her father stared from one kid to the other. He frowned so deeply Taffy thought his lips would disappear.

In a low voice, he told them, "Tomorrow, first thing in the morning, we are going to have a meeting. In the kitchen, over breakfast. Be there."

"But Dad," Russell protested, "she's the one who . . ."

"Enough! Taffy, go to bed."

Taffy pulled herself out the rest of the way from her hiding place and stood. Without looking at her father, she scurried to her room.

She knew she was in trouble. It was possible that her dad might assign extra chores. Or maybe she'd be grounded. Vacation break officially began tomorrow, and if their dad put his foot down, it could be a long summer.

As she crawled under her covers, Taffy pictured Russell squawking from the center of his bed.

When Taffy woke up, she was still smiling.

"So. Do you understand a practical joke is the lowest form of humor?"

"Uh-huh."

Their father locked his fingers and looked at them imploringly. "I don't want to punish you. I just want you to understand that there are better ways to use your energies. Read!"

"We will."

"Treat each other with respect."

"Okay."

Their dad sighed. "I've got to go to work. Russell, you clear the table. Eddy, please sweep the floor. And Taffy, I'd like you to rinse the dishes. Remember, your mother will check in with you at noon."

Pushing himself away from the table, he warned, "I'm counting on each and every one of you."

Russell and Eddy gave him the thumbs-up. Taffy stood and kissed him on the cheek.

"Good-bye, Dad. We'll be fine!"

They waved to him through the window as he backed out of the driveway. Taffy dropped into her chair. No one said a word, so she pretended to concentrate on the yellow tulips sprinkled across the wallpaper.

Cheery, Taffy decided, was a good word for the Dillon kitchen: White-ruffled curtains framed their breakfast nook; coral garden roses nodded from the center of their round oak table. In the morning sun, it seemed almost impossible that toilet paper and a Ping-Pong ball could have caused so much trouble.

"You know you had it coming," Taffy finally said.

Russell looked up. "I guess. Maybe." After a pause, he added, "You sure got even."

"Even is a good point," Taffy began, jabbing her index finger into the air. "I'm glad you see it that way—that now we're even, I mean. Plus, you did drag Eddy into it. That definitely made your joke worse than mine, but I'll go along with even, too." Taffy knew she was babbling, but Russell's narrowed eyes made her uneasy.

"When we planned the mummy joke, Russell said you'd laugh!" Eddy broke in apologetically. "I'm really sorry that I helped. Really!"

Taffy patted his hand. Eddy was a tease, but Russell was the evil joker.

A long time ago, before she and Eddy were lumped together as the "little kids," she and Russell had actually played together. But as they grew, Russell had drifted away. Then Taffy had moved on to girlfriends, and Eddy had formed his own group. They'd all spun off in their own directions and hadn't really connected much. She didn't know what to expect anymore.

After what seemed like forever, Russell cleared his throat.

"Since this is our first summer without a sitter, things could get pretty ugly if we don't listen to Dad. I *do not* want some teenage airhead watching over us. So," he looked around the table, "even though Taffy *deserves* more, I say we call a truce."

Taffy, still wary, asked, "You mean it? You really, truly swear?"

Russell rubbed the top of his head. In his Bart Simpson pajamas and Ninja Turtle robe, he looked like a rumpled cartoon. Holding up his hand, he said solemnly, "I swear."

Before he could change his mind, Taffy chirped, "Then I swear, too!"

"Great! We've got a deal!" As the three of them smacked palms, Taffy felt the knot in her stomach relax.

Getting out of the practical joke war alive was nothing short of a miracle. She knew she'd embarrassed Russell, and an embarrassed brother was a get-even brother. Thank heaven for their father's lecture!

"Okay," Russell said, "now that that's out of the way, listen up. Mom said we can fill the kiddie pool today!"

"Seriously?" Taffy grabbed a handful of dishes and took them to the sink. Their pool was just two feet deep, but it was wide and they had a lot of fun with it. Knee-high in water, they would put on goggles and race for marbles. And Taffy loved to roll in the pool, then lie on a towel and bake until every drop evaporated from her skin. Maybe Susan could come over, too, Taffy thought, although splashing around in a kiddie pool might seem babyish to her. And it would mean lying next to Susan in her French-cut, cherry-colored swimsuit with the gold lamé belt. Taffy's old peach-colored suit had a stupid ruffle across the top, which was supposed to give her body "balance" but instead make her look like a lacy hot dog. Shrugging her shoulders, Taffy dismissed the image from her mind.

It was their first day of summer and the air was warm, the sky was blue, and Russell wasn't going to kill her. It had the makings of a perfect day.

Dreamily, Taffy turned on the faucet.

A stream of water smacked her right in the middle of her chest.

"*Wha*—?" Taffy squealed. She jumped back, but the water hosed her like an unplugged hydrant. A *tat-a-tat-a-tat-a* sound rattled as it hit her ribs.

"Turn it off!" Russell bellowed.

"How—I don't—where?"

"Just turn it off!"

"*You* turn it off, you *creep!*"

Rushing past her, Russell made a grab for the faucet. The water bounced against

him until he managed to flip the handle
off. He stood, dripping; Bart Simpson
drooped to his belly button.

"Truce, huh?" Taffy spat.

Sputtering, Russell said, "You think I
did this? I *didn't!*"

"*Well I didn't either!*"

"*Then who . . . ?*"

Slowly, Russell and Taffy turned to
Eddy. From his chair, Eddy shook with
suppressed laughter.

"Pretty funny, huh?"

Russell and Taffy glared.

"It's *funny*! Come on, guys, where's
your sense of humor?"

When neither one of them answered,
Eddy began to look a little nervous. His
wide eyes darted from face to face. He
cleared his throat. "It's a joke. And I did
it before Dad said not to, so it doesn't
count. You want to see how I got it to
squirt?"

"*No!*"

"Hee, hee, hee," Eddy tittered. "I

know you're just kidding." Hopping quickly out of his chair, he made his way to the sink and pointed to the sprayer attachment. The handle on the sprayer was held down with a thick rubber band.

"See—I put a rubber band around that handle thing there."

Simultaneously, Taffy and Russell crossed their arms.

"So that made the water squirt straight out! Cool, huh?"

Taffy made a quick move to grab him, but Russell pulled her back.

"Let me go!" she cried. "That worm turned on me—"

"It's okay!" Russell told her, "We made a truce, remember?"

"Yeah." Eddy beamed. "I mean, this was a great joke—except I didn't know I'd get you, Russell. Taffy's the dish-girl. Plus, if you want to get technical, I never said truce. You guys said truce, but I didn't say the word *truce*. But now I'll say it: *Truce!*"

"That's a good point," Russell said calmly.

Frowning, Taffy stared at him. If he were serious, then he was nuts. She wasn't about to let Eddy off so easily. Cold water was trickling into her underpants while he stood grinning like a carved pumpkin!

"Hey, is Taffy going to do somethin' back on me? She looks a little . . . weird."

Russell twisted the end of his pajama top. Seven droplets of water plunked onto the floor. "No-o-o-o. Dad said not to, and I'm in charge so I won't let her do anything. Trust me."

Making a fist with her free hand, Taffy muttered, "Yeah, well, trust me, Eddy, I'd like to pop you one—" She didn't get any further before Russell yanked her through the kitchen door.

"We'll go change and be right back," he called over his shoulder.

Like a dog on a leash, Russell pulled her down the hallway, past the stone entryway, and up their spiral staircase. He was going so fast that Taffy's shoulder knocked a picture sideways; three geese on a lake hung beak-side down.

"Would you stop for a second?" Taffy cried. She carefully righted the geese, then asked, "What's the rush? I'm not stupid. You're going to do something to him, right?"

"*I'm* not, but *we* are." He looked around quickly, then said, "Wait till we're where he for sure can't hear!"

He led the way to his bedroom and ushered her inside. Craning his neck out the doorway, he checked the hall, paused, then shut the door. "Okay," he whispered, "this is a good one. The tables have turned, Taff. Now it's us against him."

Taffy felt her cheeks color. They were on the same side, for once. It felt good. As he smiled down at her, Taffy noticed how tall he'd become. A hint of sunburn washed over his freckles, and the start of an Adam's apple bobbed when he swallowed. He was twelve years old, a boy, and yet he was throwing in with her! It had always been Taffy and Eddy, the two younger kids, or Eddy and Russell, the two boys. In a way, being chosen by Russell was an honor, but . . .

"What's wrong?"

Taffy shrugged her shoulders. "Nothin'. It's just, well, we promised Dad."

"Hey, listen, let me explain the unwritten parental rule." Russell leaned forward, so close the damp cuff of his robe brushed her bare arm. "This is what they say, what all parents tell themselves before they go to bed at night." He raised his eyebrows. "Here it is: 'What I don't know won't hurt me.' "

"They don't say that."

"Sure they do. See, Mom and Dad don't care if we pull a joke as long as they don't have to hear about it. And the one I have in mind that's a guaranteed simple-to-fix-before-they-get-home practical joke. They'll never, ever know."

"I still think it would have been easier just to pop him one."

Grinning, Russell squeezed the nape of her neck. "Nah. This'll be a lot more fun.

I need your help, Taff. Whadaya say?"

Taffy bit her lip. She looked into Russell's eager face. She pictured her father, pleading with them to stop the madness. Then she pictured Eddy and his pumpkin grin.

Grasping Russell's hand, she pumped it up and down in a seesaw handshake. "I'm in," she declared firmly. "What do you want me to do?"

"So," Russell asked her, "what do you think?"

"This joke'll be perfect! Really, Russell, Eddy's going to *die*!"

They'd changed into their swimsuits, then reconvened in Taffy's room. Taffy sat on her pillow, and Russell had perched himself at the foot of her bed. Furball stalked the floor in front of them; his tail snapped back and forth like a flag in a March wind. She could tell that

Furball didn't like Russell in their room. From the way his whiskers quivered, she guessed he was jealous.

"Okay," Russell said, "do you know where to look for the stuff?"

"Yep."

"Remember, Taff, don't tip the little eraserhead off. Act casual."

"You forget the eyeball trick I played on you. I know what I'm doing."

Taffy pulled at her belt and took a deep breath. She'd borrowed one of Eddy's elastic Ninja belts and had snapped it on over her swimsuit. It was too snug, the buckle dug into her ribs, and it didn't match her suit, but it *did* make her waist look smaller.

From where he sat, Russell watched her fidget with the belt. "When's Susan coming over?" he asked.

"At about twelve-thirty. Are you going to be here?"

Russell shrugged. "I dunno. Maybe. Me and Ron are thinking of setting up a skateboard ramp at his house."

"Sounds fun. I think Eddy's going over to Brandon's."

"He is? Well, it's eleven o'clock now, so we'd better hurry with our plan. I don't want Eddy to leave before we get him."

"Yeah," Taffy nodded. She hooked her finger into the belt and stretched it away from her hip. Now she could breath on one side.

Russell cocked his head and frowned. "Why are you wearing that thing?"

"What? This?" she asked, letting go of the belt. It flipped against her waist with a *snap*. "I'm just trying to update the look of my suit. It's no big deal."

The question made her cheeks burn with embarrassment. She didn't like attention called to her beauty secrets, especially if it was Russell who was calling the attention. Next he'd probably make some smart comment about the way the belt squished her fat above and below the belt. He'd probably say her middle looked like two doughnuts stacked on top of each other. She waited, but instead,

Russell just studied his fingers.

That was new. Usually her brother couldn't resist a shot. Finally, Taffy said, "I hate how I look in this swimsuit, okay? Mom says I can get a new one after payday, but until then, I'll have to accessorize. What do you care, anyway?"

"I don't."

"Good."

She hoped that would settle it, because there was no way she could tell him the truth.

The real reason she was strangling her stomach in a Ninja belt was that she wanted a figure like Susan's, and she needed it by twelve-thirty.

Earlier, when she'd stood in front of her mirror in her bathing suit, she'd noticed that she was still absolutely straight from shoulder to hip. Hardly any change at all from the year before, except her torso was longer and the suit looked even dumber on her than before.

Susan was seven months older, and she had curves. Her mother always said that

seven months could make a big difference, but to Taffy it didn't seem *that*
long. It certainly wasn't fair for Susan to
start the summer with a great swimsuit
and curves, too.

She'd placed her hands at her middle
and squeezed hard. There, she'd thought,
that looks a lot better. If I could just hold
my waist in like that, I wouldn't look so
babyish next to Susan. And then she'd
thought of the belt.

"You know, Taffy, I think you, it, your
suit, looked fine . . . the regular way."

"Regular?"

Russell sighed. "Regular. Not different.
The old way—oh, just forget it."

Taffy couldn't help but grin. "Regular"
was as good a compliment she could hope
to get. She understood he was trying to
say she looked okay, and that was unbe-
lievable. Maybe she didn't know her
brother as well as she thought.

Meowmeow. Meowmeow. Furball
made another indignant pass in front of
them. He didn't like to be ignored.

Russell pushed at Furball's side with his toes, relieved that the moment had broken.

"Get lost, cat. You're too loud."

"Hey," Taffy said, "leave Furball alone. He's very sensitive. He thinks he's a human."

"You two have a lot in common."

"Oh, ha ha ha." She scooped up Furball and held him to her chest. "We'd better get downstairs. Eddy's going to be suspicious if we don't turn up soon."

"You're right. Let's go!" Reaching over, he smacked her palm and said, "It's show time!"

Taffy followed Russell to her door, but waited until he disappeared down the stairs. Unhooking the belt, Taffy balled it up and tossed it onto the top of her dresser. As she rubbed the groove the elastic had left in her skin, she exhaled in contentment. There was a lot to be said, she decided, for looking "regular."

5
...

The starfish on the sides of the Dillon pool had faded. Spouting blue whales were now gray, and the red crabs that seemed to crawl across the vinyl had sun-bleached to a pale pink. Sitting next to the pool, Taffy dipped her hand into the water, then let it bob along the surface. As far as she could tell, the kiddie pool didn't leak, and that was all that mattered. She and Russell were about to get even.

41

"Hey, Taffy," Eddy called out, "you gonna go in?" He was watching her from the sliding glass door that led outside to the patio. Taffy had seen him earlier, but was trying to act as if she didn't notice. In his hand he clutched a towel that said Life's a Beach.

"Oh, hi Eddy. I was just waiting for you."

Eddy crossed his arms over his chest. "You're gonna try to do somethin' to me, right? Like dunk me."

"Nah."

"Well, if I get into the pool, then I want you and Russell to stand w-a-y back. If you try and get me I'll call Mom!"

Nonchalant, Taffy said, "I swear we aren't going to dunk you. I'll do your chores all summer if your head touches water."

Eddy narrowed his eyes. "I *did* say truce, you know."

"Right. That's absolutely right."

When Eddy wore a swimsuit, his legs looked like he'd swallowed two apples and they'd caught, one at each knee. His face and the backs of his hands were freckled; the rest of his skin was Elmer's Glue white. She looked down at her fingers and began to chip at the bubblegum-colored polish. It was hard to keep from smiling. The secret she and Russell shared fizzed inside, and it was important that she not let on. She owed that much to Russell.

Russell appeared behind Eddy and sauntered to the pool. A striped beach towel was rolled around his neck, and a radio and a bag of marbles were tucked under his arm.

"Sun's up, Taffy," he said, ignoring Eddy. "How cold's the water?"

"Not bad," she lied.

"Great. This oughta be fun."

Eddy took a baby step toward them. "Taffy says she'll do my chores all summer if I get dunked."

"That's 'cause no one's gonna dunk you. You comin' in, Eddy?

Eddy shook his head. "No way. At least

not till you go in first. Maybe you guys put poison or glass or bad stuff in there."

Shrugging his shoulders, Russell stepped into the pool. Taffy followed and sat down. The freezing water made her breath catch in her throat, but she didn't let on. She gave Russell a playful splash.

"See, Eddy, it's fine."

"Hmmm," Eddy said. "Maybe."

They'd placed the pool right in the middle of their lawn, beyond reach of the cool apple tree shadows. The Dillon back-yard was enclosed by a wooden fence, and against the fence bloomed a rainbow of flowers. Red, coral, and ivory roses hovered against a border of violet and white peonies, and in between, yellow daisies splashed like bright patches of sun. In one corner their father had built a playhouse; opposite that sat a swing set with a sand-box underneath. Taffy remembered a time when she'd watched Eddy secretly bury a tooth in the sand and mark the spot with a tiny stick. He'd been worried that the Tooth Fairy was a phony. When she was sure he wasn't looking, she'd dug up the tooth herself and replaced it with two quarters. That's how it used to be, Taffy mused. Eddy and Taffy. Now, she was with Russell.

She shifted in the pool. Although the sun baked the top of her head, her legs and bottom were turning numb. "Let's start," she told Russell.

Russell emptied the bag of marbles at one end of the pool, then crawled over to her side. "You ready?"

Nodding, Taffy reached for the goggles that hung around her neck. Russell pulled his up, too.

"Get set . . . *go!*" Taffy cried. Water splashed and foamed as the two of them made a grab for the marbles that slipped through Taffy's fingers like tiny glass fish. A bony elbow, then a knee hit her in the ribs, but Taffy didn't care. Joke or no joke, this year she was going to win!

"Done!" Russell called out. "Boy, Taffy, you're getting good. Let's count 'em, but I think you won."

Eddy hopped from foot to foot. Taffy could tell he was dying to get into the game. Finally, he said, "Okay. Let me check all the swimming stuff for booby traps. If it's all right, I'll get in."

"I told you to trust me, Eddy."

Eddy squinted at the marbles, poked a stick at the towel, flipped on the radio, then dragged a foot through the water. He studied his goggles, which lay next to the pool. Everything looked fine.

"Well, okay," he said, sheepish. "I want to play now."

As he climbed in, Taffy shot a look at Russell. He winked, flashed her a quick smile back, then changed his face to serious as he dropped the marbles for the game.

"Ready?" Russell asked.

"Go!" Taffy shouted.

The three of them raced back and forth, gathering and flinging marbles until the palms of their hands and the bottoms of their feet pickled. When Russell gave her the sign, Taffy left the pool and stretched out on her towel. Little blades of grass poked around her ankles. Trying not to giggle, she scratched and waited for Russell, who threw down his towel moments later. Then came Eddy.

"That was fun!" He shivered. When he pulled off his goggles, Taffy and Russell tittered.

"What's so funny?"

Taffy couldn't help it. A laugh exploded through her nose in a loud snort.

"Nothing!" Taffy gasped. "Really!

Eddy searched one leg, then the other, then one arm, then the next. He frowned as he checked the back of his red swimming suit. "I don't see anything. What the deal?"

With an exaggerated shrug, Russell said, "I dunno. I guess we're just not used to you in makeup. Which, by the way, really brings out the color in your eyes!"

Eddy clapped his hands to his face, then ran to the sliding glass door. He could make out enough of his reflection to see deep, blue-black circles around his eyes where his goggles had been. He let out a shriek.

"Look what you did to me! I knew you'd get me! I knew it!"

Taffy rolled across the lawn, clutching her stomach with laughter.

"I'm gonna call Mom!"

Russell sprang from his towel. "No, don't! We'll all get in trouble if you tell."

"It'll come off, Eddy," Taffy told him. She sat up and hiccupped. "It's only food coloring."

With his fists, Eddy rubbed his eyes. He looked at his reflection again. The circles were still there.

"I look stupid."

"I know," Russell drawled, "but the goggle marks help."

In a voice that rose to a wail, Eddy asked, "How am I gonna get it off?"

"Come with me." Taffy got to her feet and walked Eddy to the kitchen. She dipped the edge of a washcloth into some dish soap, and began to gently rub the deep, raccoon-like marks. When she saw the look on Eddy's face, a pang of guilt shot through her.

His dark brows had pulled together so deeply they almost touched; he kept his eyes glued to the ground. Maybe he was feeling betrayed, the way she had felt when he'd turned on her.

"Come on, Eddy," she coaxed. "You'll be fine. It's really pretty funny. See, we snuck your goggles and a bottle of blue food coloring up to the bathroom, and then I painted the inside rim of the gog—"

"*You're* the one who did it?"

"Just a second," Taffy said. She rinsed the washcloth and tried again. For some reason, the marks hadn't budged. Doubling the amount of soap, she rubbed more firmly.

"Anyway," she went on, ignoring Eddy's question, "then Russell dried the goggles with a blow-dryer. You had to get wet for it to work."

"Ouch!" Eddy cried. "That's starting to hurt. Is it coming off?"

49

Taffy studied the circles. She looked at the washcloth. It was pure white, without even a trace of blue.

"Russell! Come here! Quick!"

Russell jogged into the kitchen. "What's the problem?"

"This soap isn't working. What should I do?"

"I don't know—did you try Ajax?"

"Ajax!" Eddy cried. "That sounds bad." He jerked himself free, demanding, "Let me go. I wanna see my eyes."

As Eddy darted off to the bathroom, Russell and Taffy stared at each other. In a low voice, Taffy said, "You told me it'd come off."

Russell looked worried. "Well, jeez, you can eat the stuff. You'd think it'd wash off skin."

Shaking her head, Taffy leaned on one elbow and gazed out the window.

Now Eddy was upset, and that didn't make her feel very good. Being with Russell was nice, but maybe the saying she and Susan had thought up was true:

No good could ever come from mixing with brothers. Taffy sighed. She needed somehow to fix Eddy, and then she could go over to Susan's and try on makeup, or maybe ride bikes, anything to forget about this whole, dumb practical joke war. Her eyes wandered down the tree-lined street. Suddenly, Taffy felt her stomach spring into her throat. "Oh my gosh! Look! That's Mom's car!"

"It's only eleven-thirty. What's she doing here?"

At that instant, Eddy's screams came bouncing down the walls like invisible Ping-Pong balls. *"It won't come off! Get this stuff off of me!"*

"Shut up, Eddy!" Russell yelled back. "No, wait, come here, quick!"

Eddy stomped through the kitchen door; the skin around his eyes had burned red from vigorous rubbing. The blue rings were still there.

Russell placed a hand on each shoulder; he bent down so that his eyes bored directly into Eddy's.

51

"Hurry up!" Taffy squealed. "She's pulling into the driveway!"

"Okay, Eddy, here it is. Mom's home, and it is supremely important that she think everything's fine." Yanking his sunglasses off the top of his head, he commanded, "Wear these. Don't say anything, don't do anything, and don't take them off *for* anything!"

"But—"

The door that led from the garage to the kitchen banged open; Mrs. Dillon, carrying Happy Meals and root beers, breezed in.

"Hi, kids, surprise! I brought lunch! I haven't got much time, but I thought I'd do a spot check on you three. How you doing, sweetheart?" she asked Taffy.

"Fine." Taffy flinched. Her "fine" had come out so high she sounded like a Smurf, but her mother didn't seem to notice.

"And how's the man of the house? Are things okay, Russell?"

"Great. The best. Terrific."

52

Mrs. Dillon stuck a straw in each drink. She looked up at Eddy.

"Well, don't you look cool. Isn't it a bit hard to see inside the house with those sunglasses on?"

Taffy stepped forward. She cleared her throat and said, "We, uh, we're playing rock stars. Eddy's pretending he's Stevie Wonder."

Their mother, her voice dry, quipped, "Really."

Eddy wagged his head from side to side. He grinned a huge, lopsided grin.

"Take the glasses off, Eddy."

"But, Mom . . ."

"Remove them, now."

Taffy drew her upper lip down between her teeth. She could see Russell wince. Slowly, Eddy pulled the glasses down the bridge of his nose.

"What on earth happened to you? There are blue rings around your eyes!"

Suddenly, Eddy seemed to break. He ran into his mother's soft middle and cried, "*They* did this to me, Mom. They

53

thought it was funny, and now it won't come off."

"But he squirted us!" Taffy cried. "And anyway, it was Russell's idea—"

"*My—you're* the one who—"

"Hold it! All of you! Just hold it!"

Their mother shot up a hand, as if she were a traffic cop. "Sit down!"

The three of them dropped into chairs. Eddy was in the middle. Crossing her arms, Mrs. Dillon stood in front of them. "Am I to understand that this is yet another practical joke?"

Taffy studied the floor. It was interesting, the way her baby toes curled to one side.

"Taffy!"

"Huh?"

"Your plans with Susan are now canceled. Russell, you may not have anyone in this house."

In unison, they wailed, "*M-o-m,* that's not *f-a-i-r!*"

"Oh, isn't it? How could I, in good con-

science, let another child in this mad-
house? Russell, I trusted you to take good
care of Eddy. And you, Taffy, have always
been an example to the boys."

"Eddy—" Taffy began.

Shaking her head from side to side,
Mrs. Dillon said, "Not another word. Just
look at your little brother!"

Eddy made his eyes extra big. He gazed
sadly from Russell to Taffy.

Glancing at her watch, Mrs. Dillon
quickly unwrapped the Happy Meals and
placed them on the table.

"I've got to go. Russell and Taffy, I
think being grounded one week is an ap-
propriate punishment. That includes the
TV."

Russell groaned.

"And the telephone."

"No!" Taffy gasped.

"Yes."

"Can't I make one phone call?" Taffy
pleaded. "Susan's supposed to come
over."

"Ron's waiting for me," Russell cried. "Even criminals get to make *one* phone call."

"All right. One phone call apiece. Thirty-second limit. Hear?"

She went to the sink, looked over her shoulder, and said, "Eddy, I'll take you to Brandon's house if you'd— Aaack!"

As she turned on the faucet, a stream of water sprayed Mrs. Dillon two inches above her navel.

"Who . . . how . . . ?"

Quickly their mother slammed down the handle. Eddy slipped way down in his chair until his shoulder blades touched the seat.

Their mother turned. Russell and Taffy pointed to the top of Eddy's head.

"Okay. New rules. You are *all* grounded. No TV, no phone, and *no more jokes!*"

Inside, Taffy couldn't help but smile. She was grounded, but Eddy was, too. There was justice, after all.

"Don't kill me, guys."

"No way," Taffy told him. "I don't want to be grounded any longer than I have to be. Your death would keep me here for at least a month."

Russell tunneled a rubbery fry into an egg-shaped blob of catsup. Without looking up, he commanded, "Eat your food."

Eddy saluted. "Yes, sir!"

Taffy took a half-hearted bite. Now that it was cold, the meat in her cheeseburger tasted like greasy Play-Doh. Looking from Eddy's blue-ringed eyes to Russell's angry ones, she suddenly realized what her mother's punishment really meant: She would have to be in the same house with two boys for seven long days. Without a phone.

"Being grounded's not so bad," Eddy chirped. "There's lots of stuff the three of us can do. We can play sand destructors, or Ninja Turtles, or maybe Uno—" When he saw Russell's face, Eddy stopped.

Narrowing his eyes, Russell said, "You know, Eddy, this whole stinkin' mess is your fault. You had to be the little martyr, and now I'm stuck with you. I had plans. I was supposed to go swimming with Jason. I was supposed to skateboard with Ron. You have screwed me up!"

Taffy could see Eddy color. He looked at his feet. Knitting her fingers together like a bridge, Taffy rested her chin on top and tried to think of what to do.

It had been a long time since she and Russell were on the same side, and she didn't want him to think she was going over to Eddy. It was true that Eddy was the one who'd started the war again. And he *had* tried to get around their mother by pretending he was an innocent victim. Still, it just didn't seem fair to dump all the blame on him.

A long time ago, before they'd grown and made other friends, it had been Taffy and Eddy who had teamed up, and Russell who'd been left on the outside.

She remembered how once, when she was seven years old, Russell had tried to coax Eddy away.

"Why do ya want to play with her?" Russell had asked. "Just look at what she's done to you—there's a *doll* in your bike basket. We're the men of the Dillon family. Why don't you come to the field and ride bikes with me?"

Eddy, who had just turned five, frowned until his mouth looked like a twisted berry. He'd gripped his handlebars tightly between chubby fists. "Can't she go, too?"

"Nope. This is a guy place. Sisters can't come."

"Why not?"

Russell had sighed in exasperation. He wouldn't have bothered with either of them, Taffy knew, but his best friend had just moved out of town. He'd kicked a cloud of dirt with his sneaker and said, "Just decide, Eddy."

Standing there, Taffy had felt almost invisible. She could remember the glass flecks in the cement, and how they glittered under her thongs like flakes of diamonds. A heartbeat later, Eddy said, "I want to stay here."

Without a word, Russell had jerked his bike and pedaled away.

And now, if she didn't handle this right, Russell might somehow pedal away again.

She sighed and patted Russell's shoulder. "Look," she began, "Eddy couldn't keep those sunglasses on forever—"

Russell stiffened under her hand. "Ex-cu-u-u-se me!" When he looked at her, his blue eyes blazed. "And aren't you the little brat who turned on me the exact second Mom asked about the goggle marks?"

Stung, Taffy jerked her hand free. "No, I didn't."

"Yes, you did!" In falsetto, he cried, "'Oh, Mommy, it was all Russell's fault!' Thanks, Taffy. Thank you very much."

"Well, you're the one who said that stuff would come off—"

"So? Is that the point? *No!* The point is trust a girl and die!"

Now Taffy was mad. Their tentative sprout of a friendship lay squashed. "You know what your problem is?"

"Having a sister!"

"No—your problem is you have to *blame* somebody every time anything goes wrong. You're not exactly an angel, you know!"

"Yeah! Well, neither are you. Heaven won't have you, and the other side's scared you'll take over!"

Eddy giggled. Taffy gave him a look, then tossed her cheeseburger so that it

61

spun across the table like a chewed Frisbee.

"Eddy," she asked sweetly, "how about you and me playing a game of Nintendo?"

"Sure."

Russell scowled. "Fine. You guys just leave me alone. Got it?"

"Fine!" Taffy snapped.

"Fine," echoed Eddy.

The phone in the family room was the exact color of double-chocolate fudge. Taffy stared at it, at the way light hit the brown plastic and then bent into pools of liquid gold. She gathered the cord into her hand; it curled in her palm like a nest. Lifting the receiver, Taffy touched the glowing numbered buttons and savored the sound of the dial tone. She'd survived two long days without talking to anyone on the outside world; that left five even longer days to go.

Since their big fight, Russell had stayed mostly in his room, which would have been fine except that it left her with Eddy. He stuck to her like chewed bubblegum on the sole of a sneaker. With 118 hours left in her prison term, Taffy found herself wishing she could serve her sentence in solitary.

"Go outside and play in the kiddie pool," she'd tell Eddy.

"Why don't you come? It'll be more fun."

"Nah, you go on. I'll come out in a while."

"When?"

"In a *while.*"

"When's a while?"

"A *while's* a *while.* Go *away,* Eddy!"

Whenever she snapped at him, he'd turn and look at her with his faded-but-still-there blue-ringed eyes, and Taffy would end up hanging her head and finding herself playing yet another game of fish or any number of dumb war games Eddy could think up. Now she knew there could be only one thing worse than spending the rest of her life in prison; that would be spending the rest of her life in prison with Eddy.

"Hey, Taffy, are you in there?" Eddy called from the hallway. Taffy slammed the phone back into its cradle and made a quick dash behind the family room couch. As Eddy approached, she pulled herself into as small a ball as possible.

"Taff, you've got to be here somewhere. I'm bored. You wanna do something?"

As he walked past the family room and into the kitchen, his voice floated around her.

"Hey, Taff, how about a game of checkers? Huh?" His voice faded as he went into the garage, "Taffy, where a-r-e you?"

Taffy squeezed her temples with her fingertips. Hiding from her baby brother was really low. What was happening to her? She was losing it, and she had to pull herself together fast. She needed a normal person to talk to! When Taffy stood, her eyes rested once again on the shiny brown phone. Hushing the voice that told her not to do it, that said she was grounded from the telephone and it was wrong, Taffy grabbed the receiver and punched in Susan's number.

"Hello?"

"Susan, it's me, Taffy. Listen, I'm going insane over here! I'm thinking of sitting on my floor and cutting all the hair off my Barbie dolls. Talk to me, please. I'm desperate!"

There was a pause, and then a voice said, "This is Mrs. Peterson. Do you want Susan?"

Taffy swallowed, hard. "Yes. Please."

After a moment, Susan got on the line. "Hi, Taffy. Mom says you sound really weird. Are you okay?"

"Yes. *No!*" She began to pace the room; the cord dragged behind her like a spiral tail. "I'm just sick of being trapped in this house. Russell's up in his room, I don't know *what* he's doing, and everywhere I turn Eddy's standing there saying 'Let's play reptile robots—let's play ecto gloop.' And we're grounded from the TV, too, so all I've got is a stack of books and the stinkin' radio. I—I wish you were here."

Susan chewed into the phone. Taffy must have caught her while she was eating lunch. It sounded as though she were munching an apple.

"I'll come over."

"You *can't.* I'm grounded."

"So? Your folks aren't there. I'll just sneak in the back—what's the big deal?"

"I'm not supposed to," Taffy said weakly.

"Well, you're not supposed to use the phone, and you did. There's not much difference between breaking one rule and two."

That was true. Taffy bit the edge of her lip.

"Come on, Taffy, lighten up. Your parents were really unfair. It's not your fault that they grounded you for too long."

When Taffy didn't answer, she pressed, "I've got a new issue of *Seventeen.* It's got all the summer fashions. . . ."

"I don't know. . . ."

"Fine. Just forget it. I've got stuff to do. Call me again when you feel really wild. See ya, Taff."

"No, wait!" Taffy snapped the phone cord against her bare thigh. "Come up. I'll meet you in the backyard."

"You're sure?"

"Yeah."

"Where's Russell?"

"He's upstairs in his room."

"Oh. Does he ever come down?" Susan's voice seemed to change.

"Not much. Look, if you're worried about Russell catching us, don't. Give me a minute to get rid of Eddy, and then I'll meet you in the playhouse. I'll unlock the side gate, okay?"

"Okay. See ya."

"Bye."

When Taffy hung up the phone, she noticed her heart was pounding as though she'd just run up four flights of stairs. Sneaking a friend in when she was grounded was the most daring thing she'd ever done. And possibly the stupidest. But she needed a break, and seeing Susan would be absolutely fantastic. It was worth the risk. But now she had the problem of sidetracking Eddy.

"There you are," Eddy chimed. "Where were you? I was lookin' everywhere."

Taffy raked her fingers through her hair. She had to think quickly.

"Eddy, guess what? I was upstairs, and I heard Russell, and he was making plans. I think he's trying to get us again."

"Oh, no." Eddy's mouth stayed in a small *o.*

"Yeah, Russell's mumbling to himself, and he's walking in circles, and I decided you and me are going to have to watch him. Eddy, we're gonna be spies!"

"Really?" he asked, his eyes shining.

"Yeah. Really."

A pang shot through the pit of her stomach, but Taffy ignored it. After all, Eddy was excited about being a spy, so bending the truth a little was no big deal. Actually, she was just helping him pretend. Like Susan said, it was all in how you looked at it.

"Now," she told him carefully, "I want you to sneak to right outside Russell's room, and watch him for say, twenty minutes. Then come and report back to me. All right?"

Eddy nodded eagerly. His T-shirt hung lopsided, and his thin arms poked out of the armholes like freckled sticks. He was probably the skinniest spy in recorded history.

"Taffy, you're a genius. This is better than checkers—it's perfect! Okay, so, the family room is our headquarters—"

"Right." Taffy cut him off. "But you know what? You've got to start your mission right away, or vital information could be lost." She searched around for a small notebook and a pencil, then handed them to Eddy.

"Don't let Russell see you. Be sneaky. And write down everything you see. Good luck!"

She put her hand in the small of his

back and propelled him into the hallway.

"Don't I get a code name?"

Taffy felt her molars grind. She forced a smile and said, "Sure."

"I want to be called . . . Raccoon."

"Great. A terrific choice. Go get 'em, Raccoon!"

She watched him snake down the hallway. He'd run a few steps, then stop and press his back into the wall.

Taffy shook her head. She had her own mission to worry about. Susan was waiting.

7

...

"Where have you been?" Taffy hissed.

"Changing. Let me in."

The hinges creaked as Susan stepped through the gate into the Dillon backyard.

Her just-brushed hair had been pulled up to one side and fastened with a barrette shaped like a shell. A white shirt with a seashell print was tucked into white denim shorts, and at her wrist a starfish bracelet winked in the sunlight.

Taffy looked down at her red running shorts and plain T-shirt.

"Are the guys around?" Susan asked.

"They're inside. And whisper, okay? If they find you I'll get turned in for sure. And then I'll do *hard* time."

Smiling, Susan said, "Whatever. You go ahead. I'll follow."

Taffy made a dash through the yard. She hunched way over, so that her knuckles practically dragged the ground. When she looked back, she saw Susan sprint across the lawn like a cheerleader.

Stay down! Taffy motioned with her hand. But Susan didn't seem to notice.

Once inside the playhouse, Susan set herself carefully onto the dusty vinyl floor. The scent of her Strawberri cologne wafted through the room like a sugary cloud.

"Want a Life Saver?" she asked, pulling a roll from her pocket. "They're tropical fruit."

"No thanks," Taffy told her.

In the heat, it sounded way too sweet,

but of course, she didn't say that.

Susan popped the candy into her mouth. "I've never been in here before. It's . . . cute."

"Thanks. I used to play in here lots when I was little." There was a pause. Susan patted a spot beside her. "Sit!"

Taffy dropped to the floor, crossed her legs, then changed her mind and quickly tucked her feet underneath her bottom. She hadn't noticed how dirty her toes had gotten from running barefoot.

"You know," Taffy began, "it feels like forever since I've seen you! Thanks a lot for coming."

"Sure. Except it's only been a couple of days." Susan looked over, then quickly added, "But it *is* good to see you, too."

The side of Susan's white leather sandal tapped against the floor. She sucked on the Life Saver. Her eyes wandered across the ceiling, down the paneled walls, then rested on the three-legged table pushed into one corner.

Taffy hated it when Susan did that.

73

Sometimes it seemed as though Susan had a mental list with things like missing table legs on it, and when she was done looking she gave everything she saw a score.

Missing table leg, minus three points. Taffy's dirty feet, minus five. Daring attitude, as seen by rule breaking, plus seven, with a two-point demerit for wearing tacky shorts.

"So!" Taffy declared, slapping her thighs, "how are things at your house?"

"Fine."

Susan wet her finger and rubbed the starfish that dangled from her bracelet. She polished it against her shirt and sighed. "It sure is hot in here."

"I know. Sorry."

They didn't seem to have much to say, which was odd. Usually the two of them couldn't shut up. The silence made Taffy nervous, because she felt it was somehow her job to fill the conversational spaces. As she watched Susan's eyes rove the playhouse for the second time, Taffy did what she always did; she began to talk. Fast.

"See, the thing is, I hate being locked up in my own house, especially without a phone." Taffy leaned forward so that her elbows drilled her knees. "I think your parents are so-o-o cool. Mine are like, way tough. Especially my mom."

"She's a principal—a professional kid buster. That'd be hard on anyone," Susan said.

"But what am I supposed to do? I can't get away with anything. I mean, *you've* never even been grounded. How come you're so lucky?"

Susan studied her nails. "Like I told you before, my parents just wouldn't dare."

Taffy shook her head with unsuppressed admiration.

"The only thing I can say that might help is to remember the 'divide and conquer' rule."

"Huh?"

"Well," Susan began, in her I'm-going-to-explain-this-to-a-really-dumb-person voice. "Say, for instance, my dad gets mad at me. I tell my mom, and then I try to look real sad. Then my mom gets mad at my dad, and then pretty quick my dad's mad at my mom and they forget all about me.

"A-maz-ing."

"Of course, it works the other way around, but for me, I've found Mom against Dad is the best. Anyway"—she paused to run a hand along the curve of her leg—"I was wondering, how's Russell taking all this grounded stuff?"

"I don't know. I never see him, except for maybe at dinner. I think he's staying mad at me so he won't have to deal with Eddy."

"That Russell's a pretty smart boy, isn't he?"

"I guess," Taffy shrugged. "Smart like a turnip."

Susan cocked her head to one side; her blond hair brushed her hip. "You're stuck baby-sitting Eddy full-time while Russell hides out in his room, right?"

"So?"

"So you tell me who the turnip is."

Embarrassment burned her cheeks, but Taffy managed to smile and ask, "Hey, did you bring the magazine?"

"Nope. Sorry. I forgot." Pursing her lips, which were frosted with Berry Smack lip gloss, Susan added, "And you're not going to believe this, but I've got to go to the bathroom. Real bad."

"What! You're going home already?"

"Nah, I'll just use yours."

"No way!" Taffy felt her insides squeeze into a giant lump. Susan in the playhouse was one thing; Susan skipping down their hallway was quite another.

"I'm sorry, but you just can't! What if Eddy sees you? You'll have to go to your own house."

"It's too far."

"Then use a bush!"

Susan wrinkled her nose in disgust. "Oh, give me a break. I'll be right back."

"But . . ."

"I know how to sneak. And you can't go

with me 'cause it'll be too noisy." She unwound her legs, stood, and gave Taffy's arm a quick squeeze. "Don't worry so much. Life's short."

Taffy jumped to her feet. Right then, she knew that no matter what she said, there was no way she could stop Susan. Holding her back was as practical as holding onto air.

"*Please* don't get caught," she begged.

"I *won't*. I'll be back before you miss me."

And with that, Susan was gone.

Minutes dragged by. Taffy lifted her hair and fanned the back of her neck, then reached out a toe to touch a pill bug that had crawled within reach. The bug immediately curled into a tiny, tear-sized ball.

"I know just how you feel," Taffy murmured.

Leaning over, she blew the bug across the floor. Once out of reach, the insect uncurled itself and scurried away.

"Darn it, Susan," Taffy cried, "where are you?"

Beads of sweat itched her scalp; Taffy folded an old piece of paper into accordion pleats and fanned herself, but it only felt as though she'd turned a hot blowdryer on her face. She threw down the fan and hugged her knees.

The whole thing wasn't fair! Time was ticking away while she roasted in the playhouse all by herself. What was the point of smuggling Susan over if she couldn't even be with her?

She didn't know exactly how much time had passed, but she'd watched a cloud melt across the sky, and still no Susan.

Suddenly, the sliding glass door banged open. Susan appeared and stomped across the lawn toward the back gate; her hair snapped with every indignant step.

"What are you doing?" Taffy squeaked.

Susan didn't hear.

Louder, Taffy called, "Where are you going?"

"Home."

"Why—"

"I've just—I gotta go."

Taffy hadn't known that she could run so fast. Before Susan could reach the gate, she raced across the lawn, grabbed Susan's arm, and spun her around. When she saw Susan's face, Taffy guessed the worst.

"Who saw you?"

"Your stupid brother."

"Which one?"

"Russell."

Russell! No! She was caught. Trapped. His name bounced though her head like popcorn. At that very moment, Russell might be dialing their dad at the library. Or their mother's office. Then she'd be stuck at home, by herself, for the entire summer! There was only one thing left for her to do: find her brother and beg.

"I haven't even told you what he said."

Taffy's stomach dropped even farther.

"There's a worse part?"

Tears welled in Susan's blue eyes as she

whispered, "See, what happened was, I was trying to get Furball, and he went into Russell's room, so, you know, I followed. I didn't see Russell sitting there. I swear, I thought it was safe. You should have heard what he said to me."

Susan took a wavering breath. "He said 'You're not supposed to be here. Go home, Susan.' He was so *rude*!"

Taffy's brows knit together. "Is that all he said?"

"No! He told me that . . . that he was going to get you."

Susan flicked a tear from her eyelashes. "I'm really sorry, Taff. Call me again if you get a chance. And, I've just got to tell you that you've got the *worst* brother. I *hate* him." She sniffed deeply, then disappeared through the gate.

So! Russell was going to get her. Who cared? He'd made Susan cry. In the month they'd been together, she'd never once seen Susan that upset. And no one, absolutely *no one,* got away with hurting her best friend!

81

With the curtains closed, Russell's room was dimly shadowed, yet Taffy could still make out a blanket of newspapers that covered his desk. Two mottled banana peels rested on top of the papers, along with a World War II fighting ship, a 1959 Corvette, and a plastic NASA rocket. The bite of model glue mingled with the heavy smell of ripe banana.

Russell sat hunched on his bed, his back twisted toward the door.

Taffy didn't even bother to knock.

"You know what you did?" she spat. "You made Susan cry. If you want to get me in trouble, go right ahead, but never, ever do that to my friend again!"

From where he sat, Russell announced, "That Susan's a twit."

His elbows worked against his sides. He was surprisingly calm, especially since Susan had warned her that he was going to get even. He'd mashed his hair into bushy brown clumps; from the back he looked like a wild man.

In a Transylvanian accent, Russell said, "But don't vorry, I'm not going tell Mom and Dad vat you did. You are lucky I am so nice. But I must tell you, I feel vary strange."

Slowly, Russell turned. He tilted his face to where Taffy stood.

Instead of eyes, two glowing blobs of neon green stared from his expressionless face. Still hunched, Russell rose from the bed and stumbled toward her.

"Oh, gee, am I supposed to be scared?"

Russell stopped cold. He popped the blobs of glow putty from his eyes.

"It was a joke. I heard you coming—jeez, Taffy, what's your problem?"

"Let me use little teeny tiny words, so *you* can understand. Don't you ever be rude to Susan again!"

Color spread up Russell's neck. He crossed his arms.

"Your dumb friend came in my room. If anyone should be mad, it's me!"

"She was *trying* to get Furball. She didn't know you were here!"

"Oh, right!"

"It's the truth!"

"Look, Taffy, she waltzed right in and sat down on my bed. I told her to get out. You shouldn't be playing with a girl like that, anyway!"

"Playing!"

Now Taffy was white-hot mad. Playing? As if that was all the two of them did. Susan helped her. Susan pushed her to try new things. Susan was the best friend she'd ever had! Russell had included her in on one joke against Eddy—did he think that meant they were bonded or something? Well, Taffy fumed, big deal! He would not get away with slamming her friend!

"Susan told me she came in after Furball and I believe her. I'd believe her over you any day of the week!"

"Then you believe wrong. And you know what? That Susan has been trying to turn you into a bimbo ever since you met. She wants you to be just like her."

"*What?*"

"You heard me. Ever since you've hung around Susan, you've started to change. I bet you loose one I.Q. point every hour you're with her—"

"Taffy?" It was Eddy. He stood behind her, his notebook clutched in one hand. He had a pencil stuck behind his ear.

"Go away, Eddy. This is between me and Russell."

"But, Taffy—"

"*Go away!*" She glared at Russell. "If I'm different than I used to be, I'm glad.

Susan is the best! I *want* to be like her!"

"Why? You look stupid. Your hair sticks out all over your head and you smell like bug spray."

"At least *I'm* trying to grow up. You're the one sticking glow putty in your eyes."

Russell jerked down the tufts of hair. She wasn't sure, but she thought her last line had scored a direct hit. He looked embarrassed.

"Taffy!" This time Eddy stomped his foot.

"What!" Taffy and Russell yelled together.

"I was hiding in the linen closet so I could spy on Russell, just like you told me to, and I saw the whole thing. I know what happened with Susan."

"You were *spying* on me?" Russell flared.

Taffy gulped. This was one thing she didn't want Russell to know about. She'd forgotten all about "Raccoon" and his notebook.

"That's great, Eds."

"*You* were spying on *me*?" Russell repeated. He didn't look as though he'd let the spy thing drop.

"Don't let Russell bother you. You have every right to sit in the linen closet if you want to."

"Why were you wasting your time squatting on a bunch of towels? I wasn't doing anything!"

Eddy flushed. "Well, Taffy said you were gonna get us and I needed to watch you."

"Oh, that's great." Russell smacked his palm into his forehead. "Eddy, don't you get it? Taffy was just getting rid of you so she could sneak Susan in."

"Don't believe him, Eddy." Taffy patted his arm, coaxing, "Tell me what happened. I really want to hear this." She narrowed her eyes and glared over Eddy's head at Russell. Russell glared back.

Eddy licked the eraser at the end of the pencil and flipped back three pages in his notebook.

"Okay. Susan came up the stairs and went right into Russell's room.

"Was Furball there?" Taffy asked.

"Nope. I didn't see Furball at all. So then, Susan says—"

"Are you sure Furball wasn't there?" Taffy interrupted. "He could have snuck right past you."

"No. I was watching. So *anyway*, Susan goes," Eddy peered at his notes, " 'Hi! I bet you're surprised to see me.' And Russell says, 'What are you doing here?' and Susan says, 'I was talking to Taffy, and I'm really bored. She's kind of a baby.' " Eddy looked up quickly, muttered, "Sorry, Taffy," then continued. "So she sits on Russell's bed and goes, 'Do you have a girlfriend?'—"

"Shut *up*!" Taffy screamed. "You are a *liar*!"

They must have planned this before she'd gotten there. That was the only explanation. Of course, it was obvious: Brothers always banded together against a sister. Hurt crushed her, but she pushed the pain down as far as she could. Susan would never turn on her. It just wasn't possible.

"Don't you call *me* a liar." Eddy smoldered. "That's not fair."

"Yeah," Russell retorted, "I'd call you a low-down sneak. I don't like being watched, Eddy. Why did you even *listen* to her?"

Now it was Eddy's turn to flame. His eyebrows crunched together; every freckle seemed to stand out against his pale skin.

"You just wait a second," he yelled. "*I'm* the one stuck with two of the biggest teenage whiners in town. I'm sick of both of you. Just back off!"

"I can't stand either one of you!" Taffy shouted.

"I want you both out of my face!"

"*No problem!*" the three of them screeched in unison.

Taffy and Eddy marched to their own rooms; *bang!* went Eddy's door. *Slam!* went Russell's. Not to be outdone, Taffy whipped her door closed with a wall-shattering *wham!*

All she cared about now was being left completely alone!

Furball blinked at her from the center of her bed. He might have been there all along, but . . .

Taffy shook her head. She didn't want to think anymore.

It was only when she had curled onto her own bed, with Furball clutched tightly in her arms, that she let herself cry.

...

"Hi," Taffy whispered, "is Susan there?"

"Hello? Hello?" Mrs. Peterson chirped. "I can't hear you!"

Taffy peered over the side of the couch, then slid back down into her hiding place. The phone was cradled in her lap.

"This is Taffy," she whispered, louder. "Is Susan there?"

"Oh. Taffy. Hold on, I'll get her."

Of course, there was no question in her mind at all that Susan was innocent. It was a fact. And yet . . . there was something in the way Eddy had looked at her when she hadn't believed him. . . . Taffy squeezed her eyes tight as she waited for Susan to pick up the phone. This was a risk, but she had to chance one more phone call to be absolutely certain.

"Taffy?"

"Susan, hi, it's me. Listen, I need to talk to you."

"Oh, wow, I'm so glad you called!" Susan exclaimed. "What's happening? Did they turn you in?"

"No. Neither one of them talked." She took a breath and exhaled slowly. "I don't think they're going to, either. Eddy and Russell must figure that they'll get in trouble, too. At least, that's my guess."

"You're probably right." Susan sighed. "Whatever the reason, just be glad they didn't tell. It was a close one."

Taffy nodded silently.

"So what's going on?"

Trying to make her voice as pleasant as possible, Taffy said, "Well, I know this is going to sound stupid, but—I wanted to ask you something."

"What?"

She chewed on the tip of her little finger. "Russell, well, actually Eddy, said that you went inside because . . . jeez, this is going to sound so dumb—"

"Spit it out, Taffy!"

"Eddy - said - you - said - I - was - a - baby - and - that - you - went - to - see - Russell - because - you're - in - love - with - him." Her cheeks flamed. What on earth would Susan say to an accusation like that? She didn't have to wait long for the answer. The telephone seemed to burn in her hand as Susan screamed, "I went in after your cat, and if you don't believe me, fine! Maybe you should get another friend! Maybe I should get another friend!"

"No, no, no," Taffy pleaded. "I'm sorry. Just forget it. It was a dumb question. Really, I'm sorry!"

"You should be." Susan seemed to relax a bit.

"And you're really right about Russell,"

Taffy said, picking some of Furball's hair off the rug. "He's the worst."

There was a click on the line.

"That Russell's not even cute, and he's got such an ego. The guy's so in love with himself that all he needs is a mirror to be totally happy," Susan declared.

"*What are you doing on the phone?*"

It was Russell.

"Oh, no," Susan sneered, "it's the phone police."

"Taffy, get *off* the line!"

"Bye, Taffy. Call me if you need anything, like poison or rope or something."

Susan hung up, but Russell stayed on line. Taffy could hear him breathe.

"I won't say anything about the way you're breaking the phone rule," he began in a menacing tone, "but I swear, if you talk to that bleached pinhead one more time, I'm going to call Mom and Dad and you'll be grounded till your zits clear. Got it?"

Without saying a word, Taffy slammed the receiver into its cradle.

She hoped the bang would ring in his ears for a long time.

The next morning, Taffy stared at her reflection as she brushed her teeth. Her hair hung in stringy clumps, her upper lids were puffy, and the skin underneath her eyes had darkened to a purply rose. She frowned, then spit into the sink. The strain of the blowup was definitely showing on her face.

Even her father had noticed.

"You're looking a little peaked today, pumpkin," he'd said, sticking his head into her room.

She'd been lying on her bed, scrunched into a tiny ball. Furball was wrapped around her head like a Russian hat.

"Dad, I'm begging you," she'd said, batting Furball's tail from her eyes, "this is my third day of being grounded with Russell and Eddy. It's cruel and unusual punishment. Couldn't you let me off? Please!"

"Just you?"

"Okay, okay, couldn't you let us *all*

off?" Furball flew from her head as she'd sprung to her knees. Folding her hands underneath her chin, she'd pleaded, "Have mercy!"

He'd walked over and patted her shoulder.

"Your mother and I decided on one week, and I afraid that's what it's got to be."

"But I've *paid*!"

"Honey, I know this is hard, but you three have got to learn that there are consequences to your actions. You'll stay in this house for one full week, and that's all there is to it!"

Smacking her fist into the mattress, she'd wailed, "But *Daddy*!"

He'd grinned and scratched the corner of his beard. "I think being grounded has already done you a world of good. I was noticing last night at the dinner table how polite you all were to one another. You were using phrases like 'please pass the peas,' and 'may I be excused.' What an improvement!"

Leaning over, he'd given her a peck on the top of her head. "It's time to rise and shine. Your brothers have been out of bed for an hour already."

"I don't want to get up. Maybe if I stay asleep, the time will go faster and I'll wake up free."

"I don't think it works that way. Do you want some more books?"

"No," she'd said, studying the fine lines that etched his skin.

"All right then, see you tonight."

And now, as she looked into the mirror, with a sense of dread she thought of what lay ahead.

Four more days until she was free.

Four more days with the demon brothers.

Splashing cold water on her face, Taffy closed her eyes, then blotted with a daisy print towel. Her parents had their own bathroom, but Russell, Taffy, and Eddy had to share this one.

Once she'd begged to decorate the

bathroom in delicate pink roses, but of course Eddy wanted a shower curtain crawling with bright green alligators and Russell demanded black and red stripes. They couldn't settle it, so everything stayed plain yellow.

She dropped down on the toilet and sighed. Some day, she promised herself, I'll do things my way.

Suddenly, she began to sink into the toilet bowl; her bare cheeks slid towards the cold water like the moon setting in the ocean.

"*No!*" Taffy cried. What was happening? Grabbing onto the toilet paper holder with both hands, she tried to stop the descent. She'd almost managed to pull herself out when the metal holder ripped from the wall under her weight and clattered across the floor; the toilet paper unwound in fluffy spirals.

"Oh, great!" She made a grab for the towel rack, but the reach was too much. This time she slipped dangerously close to the water line.

"Help!" she squealed. *"Somebody help me!"*

Behind the door a high, squeaky, unidentifiable voice smirked, "Gee, Taffy, you sound a little flushed. Get it, *flushed*! Ha ha ha ha ha!"

Russell? Or was it Eddy? Maybe both of them. Looking around wildly, Taffy's eyes rested on a half-empty jar of Vaseline shoved beneath the shower curtain. So! They'd greased the toilet seat. No wonder she was sinking! There was no way she could beg for help now, even if it meant staying in that position for the rest of the day!

"Taffy," the voice squeaked, "you're supposed to use *perfume,* not *toilet water*! Hee hee hee."

Taffy set her jaw; they would not win. No matter what, she would not give them the satisfaction.

Grabbing her ankles for leverage, Taffy gave a gigantic heave; she almost made it, teetering right on the edge, but at the last instant lost momentum and slid back into the bowl. This time, her bottom hit the water with an icy splash.

"Ah ha ha!"

The jolt gave her enough oomph to make it on the second try. She popped out with a loud *thwuck.*

As drops of cold water snaked down the backs of her legs, Taffy ran and unlocked the door. The hall was empty.

"Fine!" she yelled. "Get a cheap laugh! You *jerks*!"

Back inside the bathroom, Taffy threw herself against the wall. How *humiliating*! Even if they couldn't see her, they'd known she was stuck and they must have loved it. She looked first at the wide ribbon of toilet paper, then at the four holes torn from where the holder had been.

She caught sight of her reflection once again. There was a wild look in the eyes of the girl who stared back.

So, the practical joke war was back. Well, this time, she was playing alone. And this time, heaven help her brothers, she was going to win!

The Supremes. Mom'll never miss this one. Taffy studied the faded album jacket. How could her parents ever have listened to women who wore their hair teased into gigantic bubbles? Carefully, she removed the shiny black record and slipped it between the other albums stored neatly on their sides. She didn't need the music; it was the jacket she was after.

Right now, both her brothers were hiding in their rooms. She'd seen their empty cereal bowls stacked in the sink, so she knew they'd eaten breakfast. They probably figured they could stay tucked away until lunch, nice and safe. Ha! It would take more than a closed door to stop her!

Are we serious? Taffy thought as she pulled an album entitled *The Monkees* from the stack. *This has got to be one nobody'll miss. In fact, I'll be doing my folks a favor.*

She tucked the empty jackets underneath her arm and sneaked back into her room. She'd already lifted a can of her father's menthol shaving cream. The rest of the joke would be a piece of cake.

She shook the shaving cream vigorously and filled each jacket as full as she could. Little shaving cream bubbles floated through the air like tiny, mint-scented clouds.

Because she didn't know which brother had Vaselined the toilet seat, she had no choice but to get them both.

Who cared if one of them was innocent? This was war, and she was taking no prisoners.

Tiptoeing down the hall, Taffy stopped in front of Russell's room. Carefully, quietly, she slipped a loaded jacket an inch underneath his door, so that the open edge of the album lined up exactly with the door frame. Eddy's door was only four feet away; she did the same to his.

Everything was set.

Taking a deep breath, Taffy banged as hard as she could on Russell's door. Then she dashed over to Eddy's and banged on his.

"What?" Russell yelled.

"Who is it?" Eddy called.

Without answering, she zipped back to Russell's door and beat on it again. She heard footsteps. One . . . two . . . three! With a dramatic leap, Taffy landed squarely on the faces of the Supremes. *Whoomp!* An avalanche of shaving cream exploded underneath Russell's door. With a running jump, she hit the Monkees squarely on their guitars, spurting foam full force into Eddy's room. Like a racehorse, she galloped until she was safely down the stairs.

All was fair in war.

Through the open kitchen window, Taffy watched the sun slide behind clouds that had darkened to lead. It was storming in the east, and muggy wind was blowing their way. From where she stood, it looked as though giant hands had scratched the distant sky with a number two pencil.

It was three o'clock in the afternoon. Taffy took a sip from her Coke can and choked. Hot pepper coke fizzed from her nostrils. She'd left the opened can on the kitchen counter, and one of *them* had slipped a hot chili pepper into it.

Fine. No problem.

She'd already sewn Eddy's pajama sleeves shut, planted jacks underneath Russell's bottom sheet, and poked a hole in the end of the toothpaste tube. A chili pepper in the Coke can was nothing.

Rubbing her nose with the back of her hand, she cracked another container of ice and let the cubes drop into a bucket. The war was underground now, and that meant new rules.

This time, no one was telling.

And this time, no one was laughing.

I've got to strike first, I've got to get them before they get me, she told herself over and over again.

The three of them had moved throughout their house like phantoms, leaving a trail of jokes behind. It reminded Taffy of the plastic puzzles with the little squares inside, the kind where you had to move two squares over in order to push the third square up. While she was in the kitchen, Eddy could be in her room or maybe the garage. If Russell boobytrapped the family room, that left the kitchen free.

She didn't know how it would end, but of one thing she was certain: She would not quit!

A floorboard creaked.

Taffy whirled around. The kitchen was ghostly quiet.

Her eyes flew to the top page of their newspaper as it lifted in the breeze, then dropped with a whisper. Blades from the ceiling fan spun in a quiet circle. As she stood there, alert, every one of her senses tingled. The red on the Coke can seemed electric, and the flowers wilting on the window ledge smelled so pungent she could almost taste them.

This was life on the edge.

"*Wha—!*" Taffy jumped and sucked in her breath.

Furball had wrapped himself between her legs. Snaking himself across her bare calves, he mewed pitifully.

"Oh, Furball, you scared me to death."

She looked over at his dish. The blue plastic was licked clean.

"Poor baby, you're hungry. Here, I'll get you some food."

She pulled a bag of Purina Cat Chow out of the cupboard and set it on the floor. Carefully, she studied the front and then back side of the bag; she pushed it over with her toe. When a handful of pellets spilled, she squatted down to study them. Nothing. Peering into the bag, she fished around and pulled out a rubber snake.

Amateurs!

Taffy put food in Furball's dish and went back to the bucket.

Four trays of ice had been emptied into it and she'd filled it six inches from the rim with water. Okay.

She did another check to make sure the coast was clear, then dragged the bucket over to the door that lead to the garage.

Water sloshed over the rim with every step. By the time she'd towed the bucket to the door, her sneakers were soaked, but she didn't care. If this worked, it would be the best joke yet!

Now, Taffy told herself, up the ladder.

Rung by rung, she hauled the bucket as high as she could go. With a gigantic heave, Taffy lifted the bucket and set it on the top edge of the half-opened door.

Her hands hovered around its base, but

it didn't fall. Instead, it balanced perfectly!

All right! Taffy looked through the door into the kitchen. It was still empty.

As quickly as she could, she scrambled down the ladder, propped it against the wall, opened the garage door, and then ran around to the front of their house. She'd barely made it back into the kitchen before Russell showed up.

It was the first time they'd been alone, face-to-face, since the fight about Susan.

"I heard the garage door open. You can't leave," he said flatly.

"Well, gee, do I look like I'm gone?"

Russell seemed tired. Smug, Taffy noticed bits of shaving cream had dried in his hair, like large, menthol dandruff flakes.

"Having fun?" Russell asked.

"Oh, I don't know. As much fun as an airhead can have, I guess."

Russell crossed his arms in front of his chest. "Just so you know, I can keep this up as long as you."

"Fine. I'm ready."

Furball had curled himself on a pillow that had been left in front of the refrigerator.

Russell didn't like Furball much, and he especially didn't like the cat in the kitchen. Once he said that the hair Furball shed was magnetized so that it was drawn to Russell's food. No one else's, just Russell's. He claimed to have eaten twenty pounds of cat hair through the years.

It was probably because he was already mad about the joke war, Taffy decided later, that he zeroed in on Furball. Instead of arguing with her he blew up over the cat.

"What's *he* doing in the kitchen? Why'd you bring that old pillow in here? Furball shouldn't be sleeping where we eat!"

"I don't know, I—"

"He's got the run of the whole house. The only place he's not supposed to be is the kitchen."

"I *know*, and I didn't put that—"

"Sure you didn't."

Before Taffy could finish, Russell stomped over to where Furball slept. Without even bothering to move Furball off, he leaned over, grabbed an edge of the pillow, and yanked it high over his head.

Furball spun to the floor and landed daintily on his feet. He looked at Russell indignantly.

At that exact second, the bottom of the pillow opened; the entire contents of the feathers dropped on top of Furball in a gigantic feather avalanche.

Howling mad, Furball exploded from the white mound in a feather cyclone. He landed on his cat food dish and sent pellets flying. He sprang onto the countertop and streaked down its middle, knocking over a mason jar full of flowers and the can of pepper Coke as he went. The Coke and flower water mixed into a fizzing, feather soup.

"Grab him!" Taffy screamed.

110

"I'm *trying!*"

As Russell approached, arms outstretched, Furball leaned on his haunches; feathers bristled from his fur like tiny quills.

"Don't be scared," Russell purred, closing in. He was almost close enough to touch, but at the last second Furball leaped from the countertop onto the floor. He dashed between Taffy's legs and made a beeline toward the door that led to the garage.

"Furball, no!" Taffy shrieked.

Blinded by feathers that had stuck to his face, Furball missed his mark and slammed against the door with his side.

The bucket of ice water tumbled down; ice cubes, water, and the plastic bucket landed on top of the cat with a gigantic crash.

Ears flattened, wet feathers and fur plastered to his body, Furball streaked through the garage and out into the street.

Taffy ran after him. When she reached

the end of the driveway, the asphalt road, baking in the summer heat, stood empty.

Furball, who had never gone any farther away than their yard, who'd never spent the night anywhere except curled on her bed, had vanished.

The storm that had darkened the east now threatened to begin in earnest. Gusts of wind sent papers skittering down the gutter and twisted brass wind chimes into clanging spirals.

"Furball!" Taffy cried. "Come here, baby!"

"I'll go look for him." It was Russell. She could tell he was upset by the way sweat gathered at the edge of his hair.

"I don't want your help," Taffy told

him, waving him off. She ran and pulled her powder blue mountain bike from the garage. "He's my cat. I'll find him myself."

She needed to cover lots of ground, fast, and her mountain bike would be perfect. Its wide, nubby tires were made for riding through bumpy fields. Furball could be anywhere, but Taffy guessed he might have run for the tall weeds and Johnsongrass that bordered their property. At least it was a place to start.

Straddling the bike, Taffy dropped onto the seat. She frowned. For some reason the handlebars blocked her vision. When she started to pedal, her knees practically hit her ears.

"Wait a second," Russell said. His face was grim.

Grabbing the center of the handlebar with his fist, he stood in front of her and blocked her path.

"I lowered the seat on your bike all the way down for a joke. You won't be able to ride very far like that, so take mine."

"You sabotaged my bike!" she shrilled. "That's not funny. I need it—Furball's lost!"

"Sorry, Taff, when I did it I didn't think it would matter."

Wind blew a sheet of hair across Taffy's face, but she didn't raise her hand to move it.

"He's probably fine," she said. Her face contorted as she tried not to cry. "It's just that he's declawed! What if a dog chases him—he can't even climb a tree!" Taffy's voice broke. "He's cold, and he's scared. Maybe he'll run in front of a car and get hit." She pictured tires screeching as Furball darted underneath. The image made her shudder.

Eddy ran through the garage, panting, "What's going on? What's wrong?"

"Furball's gone," Russell told him. "Someone"—he paused and gave Eddy a meaningful glance—"cut open a pillow, and the feathers landed all over him and then he got dunked with a bucket of water. He really took off like a shot."

"Oh, no." Eddy's face made it clear who had done the cutting. "It was just an old pillow out of the garage," he said softly. "It was supposed to be a joke."

Miserable, Taffy added, "So was the bucket of water."

Russell turned back to Taffy. Awkwardly, he patted her shoulder. "He'll be okay," he told her. "He'll come back."

How had these jokes gotten so far out of hand? It felt like the go-round at the park, the one Taffy used to climb on when she was little. Russell would spin her round and round, slowly at first, then in dizzying circles, and she would grab the bars as tightly as she could and try with all her might to hold on.

Now, it seemed the jokes themselves were whirling them around and around. It was time to stop the ride.

The three of them looked at one another. Taffy sat up as straight as she could and pulled the hair off her face.

"Just tell us what to do," Eddy said, "and we'll do it."

This was not the time to wallow in sorrow; it was the time to move out. If she were going to cry, she'd have to do it later, because right then Furball needed her. And if there was one thing she'd learned from the practical joke war, it was that she knew how to think and carry out a plan.

"I'm going to search the field. On foot. Russell, your bike is too big for me, so you use it. Take our street and Hillside Lane, and Eddy, you go on Spring Haven and then cut over to Yermo. That way we'll cover a big square."

"We'll get him!" said Eddy.

"Let's do it!" Russell cried. He jumped on his bike and raced off.

Trotting down the street, Eddy stopped every ten paces to call Furball's name.

As Taffy began to spring toward the field, fat raindrops hit the top of her head with a *plunk plunk plunk.*

Please, God, she prayed, let Furball be okay.

Wheatgrass crunched beneath her feet as Taffy made her way to the center of the field. In the last hour, she'd been all over its five acres, calling Furball's name until her throat ached. The storm had only sprinkled before blowing on, but the wind seemed to push against her with invisible hands. The air churned with the smell of sage and dry earth.

"Furball, come on," she said, almost to herself. "Where are you?"

Every time she rounded a hump of earth, she expected to find Furball crouched, scared and shaking, but the grass was always empty. The knot in her stomach clamped tighter and tighter.

A voice blew in from the distance as a faraway shape called to her, " . . . found . . . got Furball."

What! The blood came back to Taffy's legs as she ran closer and closer toward the figure.

When she was near enough, she saw that it was Eddy. He held something

118

tightly in his arms. "I found him!" Eddy cried. This time his voice reached her loud and strong. "Look, Taff. Here he is!"

Clutching Furball under the forearms, Eddy held up the cat. Furball stretched from his shoulder all the way to his knees.

Absolute joy and relief washed through her. Furball was okay! She ran the rest of the way faster than she knew she could and grabbed the cat into her arms.

"I was so worried about you!" she cried, panting. "Are you all right? You scared me!" She hugged him close and buried her face into his coat. Feathers still clung to his fur, which had dried into stiff clumps. Furball began to purr in her arms. He seemed to think nothing out of the ordinary had happened.

"Thanks, Eds," she said, kissing the top of his head. For once, Eddy didn't rub the kiss off. Instead, he beamed.

"I told you I'd find him! He was underneath a porch and I almost didn't see him, but then I saw his eyes glow. You know what? He wouldn't even come to me when I called. I had to crawl in and get him."

"He was probably mad, the little bum. Really, Eddy, thanks a lot for looking."

"No problem. We'd better go find Russell, though, 'cause he's riding all over. The last place I saw him was on Bell Street."

Cradling Furball like a baby, Taffy fell into step beside Eddy. She picked feathers off the cat's coat as they went.

Eddy rubbed a grass stain off his elbow and mused, "Hey, do you remember the time Mom burned the fish and she said we still had to eat it, so we sneaked it to Furball instead?"

"Yeah! And Furball upchucked right at Dad's feet. We really caught it then."

Eddy smiled. "We sure used to get into trouble."

"No, we didn't," Taffy protested, shifting Furball higher in her arms. "Not that much."

"Oh, yes we did. You must've just forgot. Like that time we drew all over the driveway with my crayons."

"Oh, yeah, I haven't thought about that in forever! But that was Russell's fault. He *said* they were the same as chalk."

She shook her head. It was hard to believe she could ever have been so dumb. "Hey, Eddy, I just thought of one. Do you remember when I was six, and you were about four, and the two of us took Russell's goldfish for a walk? We put the whole glass bowl on his skateboard and wheeled it down the driveway—"

"Yeah," Eddy broke in, "poor Golda."

"Umm. That was bad."

From the corner of her eye, Taffy studied Eddy. There must have been bushes around that porch, because his hair bristled with small green leaves. He really was kind of cute, in an eager, puppy-doggy sort of way.

And surprisingly loyal. Here they'd been in a fight, and he'd done everything he could to save Furball. A question teased at the corner of her mind. Would Susan have done the same?

"I—I hope you're not mad at Russell anymore." Eddy said, interrupting her thoughts. "Or me, either."

"I'm not. I promise. Except, I do want to know *one* thing. Who did the toilet seat? Was that you?"

Eddy nodded modestly. "I was a little steamed 'cause you called me a liar—" Eddy quickly swallowed the word, then said, "Well, anyway, I thought that up all by myself. Russell didn't even know. But your shaving cream one was just the best. Where'd you learn that?"

"I heard Mom tell Dad about it when she thought no one was listening. She said she did it to her sorority sisters in college all the time."

"Mom?"

"I know. It was a shock to me, too."

Furball was getting heavier and heavier, so Taffy threw the top part of him over her shoulder. His front paws hung down her back, and his head bobbed with every step.

They walked on in silence.

Just ask him, a voice inside Taffy whispered. She knew this was a perfect opportunity to talk to Eddy and find out what really happened in Russell's room that day. But she couldn't. She wasn't sure she wanted to know.

Taffy squeezed Furball and blurted, "What did Susan *really* say when she went in there?" Her eyes widened. Where did that come from? It seemed as though someone else possessed her lips, and now her words, like blown bubbles, were out floating in the air. Oh, well, at least she'd asked.

Eddy looked at her, his face solemn. "You really want me to tell you?"

"Uh-huh. I guess I do."

By the time they found Russell on Verano Loop, Taffy knew exactly what had happened. She still could hardly wait for their punishment to be over, but this time it was for a different reason.

She intended to confront Susan, face-to-face.

12

"Is Susan here?"

"Taffy. Hello," Mrs. Peterson said. Mrs. Peterson was one of the thin mothers. Her smooth blond hair had been cut in an expensive salon style, but Taffy didn't like it much. Even though Mrs. Peterson tucked one side neatly behind her ear, the hair kept falling to the front of her face. Instead of using a barrette, Mrs. Peterson seemed to think it necessary to toss her head every few seconds.

"Yes, Susan's here but she's on the phone with a friend"—toss—"so why don't you wait in the den"—toss. "I'll go tell her you're here." Double toss.

"Thanks," Taffy murmured.

She already knew the way to the den, and Mrs. Peterson didn't bother to take her there. She watched as the woman disappeared down the hallway. Her own mother's gait seemed much more solid and reliable than Mrs. Peterson's glide.

Once inside the den, Taffy perched on the edge of a cream-colored leather chair and waited. And waited. Her thoughts drifted to Black Wednesday, the name she'd given to the day Furball ran away.

"I knew we'd catch the little fleaball. Way to go, Eddy!" Russell had said when they'd finally caught up with him. He'd rubbed Furball between the ears, and as the cat rumbled with contentment Russell bent his ear close and said, "What's that? Oh. Furball says, 'I got feathers! I don't know if I'm a cat or a bird, I'm so confused.'"

Maybe, Taffy grinned, he liked that cat better than he let on.

Russell gave Furball a final, vigorous rub, then stood and straddled his bike. "Well, guys, let's get home. It's been a long day."

"No kiddin'," said Eddy.

As Russell pedaled ahead, Taffy'd noticed how muscle thickened down the curve of his back. He used to be just skin and ribs, but not anymore. Like her, he was growing up.

I need to talk to him, she'd told herself. She'd looked over at Eddy, who'd taken a turn carrying Furball. The cat seemed to sag in his arms.

"When are you going to tell him?" Eddy asked.

"As soon as we get home. And don't forget that you *promised* not to say anything about our conversation."

"I won't—"

" 'Cause I need to handle this myself. I'm going to wait till just the right moment."

The blue circles around Eddy's eyes were almost gone now. Nothing remained except faint shadows that made him look a little older, and wise. "You're stalling," he said simply.

"No, I'm *not*! It's just, I've got to say this when the time is right."

"When's that going to be?"

"When we get home—I want to talk to him alone. Just let me do this my way, okay?"

But when they'd walked into the kitchen, the three of them had stared in disbelief. Their mouths dropped at what used to be the tidy Dillon kitchen.

Water, Coke, cat food, and feathers oozed across the floor like a mottled mud slide. A layer of gray-white feathers curled gently on the countertops. A few had even floated to the kitchen table. Furball jumped from Eddy's arms and daintily picked his way though the mess.

Reverent, Eddy said, "Wow. If Mom sees this we can all kiss the whole summer good-bye."

"And I just thought of something," Russell added. "The upstairs is almost as bad."

Taffy's eyes riveted to the clock. It was four-thirty. Their mother would be home in forty-five minutes.

This time it was Russell who took command.

"Taffy, you get the mop. Those feathers are full of water, so they should mush into a pile. Eddy, you do the counters and scrape up the cat food. I'll take the upstairs."

"Oh, jeez, don't forget I pulled the toilet paper holder out of the wall," she reminded him. "Can you fix it?"

Russell watched the clock's minute hand click forward. "I'll get the screwdriver."

"And just as soon as Eddy's done, I'll send him up to degrease the toilet seat. That sucker's deadly!"

She tossed the rubber snake at Russell. He caught it with one hand. "We can do this, guys," she told them. "We have to."

They'd gone down the list, fixing, wiping, brushing, cleaning, right up until the time their mother walked through the door.

If their mother knew something, she never said. The only comment she'd made came the next morning, when she'd asked, "How on earth did *feathers* get in my toaster?"

But Taffy never did find that "right moment" to talk with Russell. Maybe she hadn't really tried. Over the next three days, she convinced herself that the best thing would be to wait until after she'd confronted Susan. That way, she'd have all the facts.

Taffy stood in the Peterson den and began to pace. The room was decorated exclusively in white, and Taffy was afraid that if she sat too long, she might leave some sort of mark. A matching leather couch rested on a thick, ivory-colored rug, and the end tables, coffee table and desk were all antique white. A dozen white tulips nodded from a crystal vase.

"Hey Taffy!" Susan called, breezing into the den at last. "How does it feel to be on the outside?"

Taffy whirled around to face Susan. "Lots better."

"That's great. It's so good to see you. That's a cute top, but do you know what that outfit needs?"

"Nothing," was Taffy's abrupt reply.

"Oh! Well, that's not exactly what I was going to say, but I can tell by your face this isn't the time."

She plunked herself on the matching leather sofa. Her hair had been French braided, and the golden strands from the top of her head made a zigzag pattern against the dark honey blonde underneath. "Sit," she commanded.

"No, thanks."

"I bet you'd like to do something today." Susan paused, smiled, then went on. "But, darn it, I forgot your week was up, so I've got stuff lined up till tomorrow. How about Wednesday? You want to go shopping?"

"I'm busy."

"Really?" Susan looked surprised.

"Yeah, really. In fact, I'm all booked up. Totally. The only reason I'm here is because I want to talk to you about Russell."

Clouding, Susan asked, "What about him?"

This was the moment Taffy had been waiting for. She'd rehearsed her lines a hundred times, but with Susan staring at her, the words dried up. Taking on someone like Susan was hard, but, she realized, anger creates its own courage. Crossing her arms, she blurted, "Why did you lie to me?"

Susan's eyes flashed. "Are we back to that? I thought we settled it. I went in after Furball. How many times do you want to hear this?"

"I don't want to hear that part ever again. What I want to hear is the truth."

"Furball—" Susan began.

Taffy cut her off with the wave of her hand. She stepped closer and said, "Eddy was in the linen closet. He heard everything. He even wrote it down. So let's start over. Why did you lie to me?"

Stunned, Susan opened her mouth, thought better of it, then shut it again.

"Well?"

Like a well-oiled machine, Susan switched gears. She tipped her chin and quipped, "*Lie* is such an ugly word. Let's just say I put a spin on the truth." She giggled. With no response from Taffy, the giggle died out like the ember on the end of a match.

"I don't want to call it anything except what it is," Taffy said bluntly. "So let's just call it a plain old lie."

"Jeez, Taffy, you don't have to get so defensive. Why is this such a big deal?" Susan had a gold necklace on, and as she spoke, she pulled the chain into her mouth. "Okay, okay, I talked to Russell. So what?"

"So what? So *what*? Russell's my brother, and you made me choose *you* over *him*. I even called Eddy a liar, 'cause I didn't think a friend would do that to another friend. I believed you instead of my own brothers!"

Throwing herself into the sofa, Susan whined, "Give me a break. If I'd told you the truth you would have felt bad, and I didn't want to hurt your feelings. I only lied to protect you—"

"Oh, just stop," Taffy cut her off. "You always have a smart answer, but you can't worm out of this." Holding up her fingers, she counted off, "You bad mouthed me, to my *brother,* then you tried to get him to like you, and then you topped it all off by lying to me. That's sleazy, Susan, no matter how pink your nail polish is."

Susan's wide, pale eyes followed Taffy's every motion. She actually seemed nervous. That was a twist; Susan, nervous around her. The truth must have its own sort of power.

Draping her arm over the side of the couch, Susan tried to change her expression into a nothing-bothers-me-at-all look, but Taffy wasn't fooled.

Susan, who did everything to make

herself perfect on the outside, had some pretty ugly things on the inside. She knew it, and now Taffy knew it, too.

Tossing her head exactly the way her mother had, Susan asked, "Am I supposed to care about this? Because I really don't. I mean, I've helped you with your clothes, and your makeup, it's like I really *improved* you, and then look what happens. Well, go ahead, just try and find another best friend."

Taffy spun on her heel and walked to the doorway of the den. Without turning around, she said, "I already have."

"Why aren't you gone?" Taffy asked.

Russell was in the kitchen, hunched over a bowl of cereal. It was ten o'clock in the morning, and so far he'd already eaten a large stack of pancakes and two hard-boiled eggs. If there's one thing that boy can do, Taffy thought, it's eat.

"I'm still here 'cause Jason's stuck at the dentist's, but he should be back pretty quick and then we're going to the pool. Eddy was out of here before eight." He paused and took another bite. "Where were you?"

Taffy felt her heart leap. There were no more excuses. Now was the time.

"I was—I was at Susan's."

"Oh." Russell took another spoonful of cereal and began to read the back of the box.

"We had a fight."

"Hmmm."

"About you."

Now Russell looked up. He stopped chewing.

"I know everything you said about Susan was true. Eddy told me the whole story when we were walking home that time with Furball. I'm really sorry I called you a liar."

Russell shrugged. "No problem. Let's just forget it."

"No. I've still got to say this part. Eddy said that you told Susan to lay off of me, and that if I turned into a . . . " Taffy stopped and searched for the words.

"A mutant Barbie doll—"

"Yeah, if I turned into a mutant Barbie doll, you'd hold her personally responsible. Did you really think I'd change into something like that?"

Russell colored. "Look, you didn't do any of that primpy stuff until you started hanging around Susan. I just think—listen, you don't have to change for anybody."

Taffy tried to stifle a smile, but didn't make it.

Hotly, Russell said, "This isn't funny!"

"No, no, no. I think it's really sweet—"

Russell made a gagging noise, so Taffy changed her word. "I mean *nice,* that you think I should stay the same. But even if I don't like Susan anymore, I still like some the things she showed me. Anyway, I really appreciate your sticking up for me. Thanks."

"You're welcome. Now can we stop talking about it? I just ate."

"Sure," Taffy told him.

She looked out the window at the blue sky. The sun had already warmed the air to eighty degrees, and the wind had died to a gentle breeze. It would be a perfect day to swim.

"What are you going to do now?" he asked her. "Got any plans?"

"I don't know, maybe I'll pop some popcorn and watch TV, or I might actually finish one of those ecology books Dad brought home." Under her breath, she added, "That ought to make him faint. And *then* I was thinking of calling some kids I haven't talked to in a while. Just to see what they're up to."

He drained the milk from his bowl and wiped his mouth with the back of his hand. "Hey, if you don't overdose on TV, *Frankenstein*'s on 'Creeper Theater' tonight. You want to watch it?"

"I guess. But *no* toilet paper."

"Nah, it's been done. Besides, this is *Frankenstein*."

"Then no bottle caps on your neck, no grunting—"

"No promises!" he said darkly.

Taffy gave him a sly smile. "Then I

guess I don't promise, either."

He threw himself back from the table, raised both hands and cried, "Okay, okay, I give. I swear, if I'm ever stuck in this house again for a whole week with you guys, one of us won't make it out alive."

Rolling her eyes, Taffy turned her attention once again to the outside. The wind chimes made soft clangs, like small, tubular bells. Furball was curled on a patio chair, contentedly soaking up sun. On the street beyond, Eddy and his friend Brandon practiced wheelies on their bikes.

"Hey," she said, squinting, "is that Jason out there?"

Russell jumped from the table and looked out. Sliding the window open, he called, "All right, Jase! No cavities, huh?"

Jason poked the air with his thumb and grinned.

Grabbing his towel and sunglasses, Russell made a dash for the back door.

"See ya, Taff," he called over his shoulder.

Russell didn't invite her go with him, and she didn't ask.

Taffy looked around the sunny, empty kitchen. She picked one last feather from the top of the flour canister and blew it off her fingertips. Then she headed for the phone.

The practical joke war was over.